fly away

Patricia MacLachlan

fly away

MARGARET K. MCELDERRY BOOKS
New York London Toronto Sydney New Delhi

MARGARET K. McELDERRY BOOKS

An imprint of Simon & Schuster Children's Publishing Division

1230 Avenue of the Americas, New York, New York 10020

MARGARET K. McELDERRY BOOKS is a trademark of Simon & Schuster, Inc.

For information about special discounts for bulk purchases, please contact Simon & Schuster Special Sales at 1-866-506-1949 or business@simonandschuster.com.

The Simon & Schuster Speakers Bureau can bring authors to your live event. For more information or to book an event, contact the Simon & Schuster Speakers Bureau at 1-866-248-3049 or visit our website at www.simonspeakers.com.

Book design by Debra Sfetsios-Conover

The text for this book is set in Baskerville MT.

Manufactured in the United States of America

0114 FFG

10 9 8 7 6 5 4 3 2 1

Library of Congress Cataloging-in-Publication Data

MacLachlan, Patricia.

Fly away / Patricia MacLachlan.—1st ed.

p. cm.

Summary: While in North Dakota helping her Aunt Frankie prepare for a possible flood, Lucy finds her voice as a poet with the help of her two-year-old brother, Teddy, the rest of their family, and a few cows.

ISBN 978-1-4424-6008-9 (hardcover)

ISBN 978-1-4424-6010-2 (eBook)

[1. Family life—Fiction. 2. Brothers and sisters—Fiction. 3. Floods—Fiction. 4. Poets—Fiction. 5. Cows—Fiction.] I. Title.

PZ7.M2225Fly 2014

[Fic]—dc23

2012040995

For Sofia, who first sang the song—
For Nicky, who sings it too.
Love,
P. M.

My thanks to Anne Ramsey, Director of the Dalcroze School at the Lucy Moses School in New York City, who adapted "The Birdies Fly Away" song from Engelbert Humperdinck and graciously gave me permission to use it. My thanks also to Haeeun Shin, talented Eurhythmics teacher at the Concord Conservatory of Music in Concord, Massachusetts, who taught the song to my grandchildren, Sofia and Nicholas.

—Patricia MacLachlan

fly aWay

The Birdies Fly Away

The birdies fly away, and they come back home.
The birdies fly away, and they come back home.
Fly away, fly away
All the birdies fly away,
The birdies fly away, and they come back home.

chapter 1

Secrets

We drive across the Minnesota prairie in our old tan and green Volkswagen bus. My father does not believe in new cars. He loves the old Volkswagen with the top that pops up like a tent. He can take the motor apart and fix it himself.

In the way back are neat wooden

framed beds for sleeping. In a pen are Mama's chickens: Ella, Sofia, and Nickel. Mama loves them and never goes away for long without them. My younger sister, Grace, sits in her car seat next to me. In back of her is Teddy, the youngest, with his stuffed beaver.

My father, called Boots because he wears them, is driving, listening to opera on the radio. It is *La Traviata*.

Misterioso, misterioso altero . . .

I know it well. If a conductor dropped dead on stage I could climb up there and conduct.

Now here is something abnormal. I can't sing. When I open my mouth nothing happens. I know the music, but I can't sing it. I can only conduct it.

My father went to Harvard. His parents expected him to be a banker like his father. In secret he planned to be a poet.

But then he discovered cows. He became a farmer.

He loves cows.

"They are poetry, Lucy," he tells me. "I can't write anything better than a cow."

Maggie, my mother in the front seat, wears headphones. I know she is listening to Langhorne Slim. She loves Langhorne Slim as much as my father loves opera. And I know *her* secret. She would like to sing like Langhorne Slim. She would like to *be* Langhorne Slim.

If you've got worries, then you're like me.
Don't worry now, I won't hurt you.

My younger sister, Gracie, ignores the opera and my mother's bopping around in the front seat. Gracie sings in a high perfect voice, fluttering her hands like birds.

"The birdies fly away, and they come
back home.
The birdies fly away, and they come
back home."

I turn and look at my little brother, Teddy. He smiles at me and I know what that smile is all about.

In his small head he is singing the "Fly Away" chorus in private so no one can hear.

Fly away, fly away,
All the birdies fly away.

I smile back at him.

This is our secret because Teddy wants it that way.

I have known for a long time that Teddy can sing perfectly in tune even though he is not yet two. We all know he doesn't speak words yet. But only Teddy and I know that he sings. He doesn't sing the words, but sings every song with *"la la la."* He sings to me every night, climbing out of his bed, padding into my room in the dark. He sings a peppy "Baa, Baa, Black Sheep," ending with a "Yay" at the end with his hands in the air.

"La La La La
LaLaLaLaLa.
Yay!"

He sings a soft, quiet "All the Pretty Horses." *"La, la, la."*

I made a mistake once and told them all—Boots, Mama, and Gracie—that Teddy can sing. They didn't believe me. And of course Teddy wouldn't sing for them. Only for me.

"I've never heard Teddy sing," says Gracie.

"He can't even talk yet," says Mama. "How could he sing?"

Teddy has music but no words.

I have words but no music.

We are a strange pair.

And here is *my* secret: I am planning to be a poet. I have written thirty-one and a half poems. Some are bad. They are bad hideaway poems. I plan to get better and publish better poems and buy Mama more chickens and take Boots to see *La Traviata* at the opera house in New York City, wherever New York City is.

When I get to be a poet Boots will be pleased.

He will be proud.

And one day, for him, I will write a poem as beautiful as a cow.

chapter 2

Cow

The reason we have all been loaded into the old bus is that we spend part of every summer with Aunt Frankie in North Dakota. Everyone calls her Frankie. Her name is Francesca, but she says that is pretentious. That is the first time I ever heard the word "pretentious," and I've been looking for a time to use it ever since. It is much too long for a poem.

Frankie, who Mama says is as "old as time," lives far out in the middle of the universe. She lives by a big river that floods in the rainy season. It is now the rainy season, and Boots says it will flood while we're there.

"Frankie will need our help even though she doesn't think so," says Boots.

"She is so stubborn," my mother complains.

Boots looks at me in the rearview mirror. It is like looking into my eyes, we look so much the same.

He smiles.

"Who else is stubborn?" he asks.

"Mama!" says Gracie.

Frankie has a few milking cows she milks every day, but leases most of the higher meadowland for other people's cattle.

There are few trees, no mountains, just miles and miles of prairie grass and gophers and sky.

And the river.

Frankie's house is the house where Mama grew up. Mama loved it and hated it at the same time. She always cries when we get there and cries when we leave. Maybe one day I'll understand that.

"It sounds like 'the birdies fly away and come back home' to me," I once said to Boots.

"You're very right," he said, peering at me as if I'd said something important.

At dusk we find a place to stop for the night. It is a state park hill with an open field, bordered by a farmland fence. Mama lets Sofia, Ella, and Nickel out of their crates and spreads chicken feed on the ground for them. They flap their wings and mosey around, eating and strutting. My mother and father get out their chairs and their small stove. They set up their tent near a tree. Gracie, Teddy, and I always sleep in the car beds, Teddy in the middle. Mama and Boots could sleep in the bus, but they love their small domed tent.

"Why can't we stay in a motel?" Gracie asks. "Trini's family goes to a motel with a pool and dining room and miniature golf course where a little volcano goes off if you get a hole in one."

I know what Boots is about to say. I've heard it many times. I've even written a poem about it. Gracie has heard it before too, but she is young enough to think the answer may change when she asks to stay in a motel. She'll know better one day.

Motel Room

Where's the river?
Where's the sky?
Can't see the clouds—
Or bluebirds fly by.

Boots waves his arm.
"In a motel you wouldn't have this great view," says Boots. "You'd have four

walls with boring paintings."

"Maybe a motel would have a pool," said Gracie.

"Maybe we'll find a river," said Boots.

Can't smell the flowers,
Can't smell the sea—
Four walls and bad art
Is all that you'll see.

I take Teddy for a walk in the meadow. He reaches up and takes my hand with his tiny hand. His hand is warm. He wears red sneakers and a faded T-shirt with a green fish on it.

Suddenly Teddy stops. He is staring at something. He points.

"Cow," he says.

"Teddy, you said cow!"

As far as I know Teddy has never said cow. But he says it as clear as light. He says it again.

"Cow."

"Mama!" I shout. "Boots! Teddy said cow!"

Mama waves. Boots and Gracie come quickly across the field and look where Teddy is pointing. Far off, at the fence, stands a cow. It is a kind of cow I've never seen. Ever.

"Oh, my." Boots's voice is strange. "Oh, my," he repeats.

"Cow," says Teddy again.

"Oh, my," says Boots again.

I feel like I'm in a strange echo chamber.

Boots starts to walk toward the fence, then comes back to scoop Teddy up in his arms. He beckons for us to follow.

At the fence is a very large cow. She is beautiful and black, with a wide white stripe around the middle of her. My breath catches. Maybe Boots is right after all. That he couldn't write anything more beautiful than a cow. Maybe no one can.

"Cow," says Teddy.

"I know that," I say, then I laugh because it is Teddy I'm answering.

"Dutch Belted," says Gracie. "Boots's cows are mostly Holsteins or Guernseys," she tells me.

Gracie has a chart at home of all the cow breeds. She opens her notebook and takes out a pen. She begins to draw the cow.

"I've never seen one," says Boots. He puts his hand across the fence and the cow moves back quickly. Then, after a moment, she comes back so Boots can rub her head.

"Beautiful," says Boots. "Beautiful Dutch Belted."

"Cow," says Teddy.

"Yes, Teddy," says Boots. "Dutch Belted."

Teddy reaches his hand over the fence and rubs the cow's head, imitating Boots. The cow's tongue comes out, long and rough, making Teddy jump.

The sun goes down behind the faraway line of trees. Two more Dutch

Belted cows move toward us, probably hoping for grain.

"Cow," whispers Teddy, putting his arm around Boots's neck.

Nighttime. Grace is sleeping. She is always first to go to sleep. There are stars out in the black sky and I can see the glow of the lantern light in Mama and Boots's tent. There is a slice of moon above the trees.

"See?"

It is Teddy's little voice next to me. That's the only part of my name, Lucy, that he can say—the "see" of Lucy.

"Teddy," I whisper.

"Cow," he says.

"Cow," I whisper.

His eyes gleam in the dark. I know he's

going to sing now. *And he does. He sings the song perfectly, all the la la's in tune. I hear the words in my head.*

"*Fly away, fly away,*
All the birdies fly away."

I reach over and take his hand.
And we sleep.

chapter 3

Night Song

In the morning it is drizzly and dreary. Boots is listening to the weather forecast on the car radio.

"More rain and storms today," he says, worried.

Mama packs up the chickens. I help Gracie into her car seat. She clicks herself in. I lift Teddy into his seat back by the chickens. I click him in.

He points to the chickens.

"Cow," he says.

Gracie and I laugh.

"Chickens," says Gracie. "I'll draw you one."

She takes out her paper and markers and quickly draws a very good chicken. She hands it to Teddy.

Teddy smiles at her.

"Cow," he says happily.

"I think that for Teddy 'cow' means 'Look! There's something!'" I tell Gracie.

Boots stows the tent in the storage under the beds. The car is packed.

Boots starts up the car.

"Ready?"`

"Ready," says Mama. She puts on her headphones.

"A day and a half to go," says Boots.

Boots turns on his tape. Today it is *Aida*, the triumphal march. Somewhere in act 2. Boots once told me that when the opera is presented there is a huge parade of people and animals, sometimes elephants, camels, and horses. Maybe I'll take Boots to see *Aida* when I'm a rich poet. There aren't any elephants or camels in *La Traviata*.

We drive off in the mist. Gracie leans over and points to Teddy. He is keeping time to the music on his car seat. If he hears it enough, he'll be able to sing it.

We drive off down the highway. I take out my writing book and my pen.

I stare at the blank lined page. I feel the same way about a blank page that my Mama feels about her old home in North Dakota. I love it because it is fresh and clean. I hate it because I have to fill it.

I think about the shining coal-black cow with the surprising white circle around her middle.

I write a line.

Ring-Around cow.

I look at it so hard my eyes blur.

Outside the car window horses run by the fences.

"Cows!" yells Teddy.

"I have to go to the bathroom!" calls Gracie.

I sigh.

It's going to be a long drive.

It is late afternoon when the storm starts, rain coming down softly at first, then harder. There is thunder and lightning, the lightning coming down to the land all around us. The wind picks up.

Teddy sleeps through the storm in his car seat, a sweet peaceful look on his face. Flashes of lightning light up his face, but still he sleeps.

Then there is a new sound.

Mama takes off her headphones to listen. Hail begins to fall on the roof of the van, bouncing off like small stones at first, then harder, so hard that Boots can't hear his music. Boots pulls off the road, peering through the windshield. He parks under an overhang by gas pumps. The sudden quiet wakes Teddy.

"See?"

"It's all right, Teddy. You can go back to sleep."

Teddy puts his thumb in his mouth and closes his eyes.

"I'll fill the gas tank and then we'll decide what to do. We can't drive in this."

Mama peers out.

"No, we can't. It isn't safe."

Boots pumps gas and runs into the gas station. I can see him talking on the cell phone. After a bit he comes back with crackers and cheese, some bottles of cold water, and cookies.

His hair is wet with rain.

"I called Frankie and told her we'd be there for her," he says. "She said stay away. She doesn't need help."

"Of course she did," says Mama. "Frankie is stubborn."

Boots smiles.

"She told me to turn around and go home!" he says.

"What did you say?" I ask him.

"I told her okay, we'd go home," says Boots.

"You didn't tell the truth," says Gracie.

"True. I didn't want Frankie to worry."

"That woman," says Mama.

Boots takes her hand.

"That woman," he whispers, making Mama smile.

"All the motels are full," Boots says, handing out snacks.

"We can't set up our tent in this," says Mama.

Boots shakes his head.

"The owner of the gas station says there's a park with a pavilion down the road. We can park under it for the night."

"And food?" asks Mama.

"We'll get hamburgers just before we get there."

"Where will you sleep?" asks Gracie, yawning already.

Boots drives off, the noise sudden and loud again.

"We'll all sleep in the car!" says Boots with a laugh. "It will be fun!"

Mama laughs too.

"Even the chickens?" asks Gracie.

"Even the chickens," say Mama and Boots together, laughing.

My parents are crazy.

We eat hamburgers and Teddy discovers pickles.

"Mo," he says. "Mo."

So we hand our pickles over to him.

We park under the pavilion and put down the front car seats.

The hail is still strong on the pavilion roof, but when Mama and Boots get in their sleeping bags, the chickens between them, it is fun.

And when Boots turns out the lantern and it is dark, Teddy leans over close to me.

"See?"

"Teddy."

And he sings to me. He sings "Twinkle, Twinkle" without words, and "Fly Away," the whole song.

But the noise of the hail is so loud that no one else hears.

I'm glad.

I like that this is our secret, Teddy's night song.

Teddy's and mine.

chapter 4

Red River

The next day there is light mist and sun at the same time. We drive with a huge rainbow off in the horizon.

"Rainbow, Teddy," says Gracie. "See?"

"Cow," say Teddy and Gracie and Mama and Boots at the same time, knowing what he will say.

Teddy thinks it is very funny that we all say the same thing, so he says it again.

"Cow!"

"I wish he'd say more words," says Mama. "He's a late talker. You all spoke early."

"Early and often," says Boots.

"He talks in his own way," I say.

Mama turns to look at me.

If only Mama knew.

"We all have things we can do and can't do," says Boots.

"Well, *I* can't *sing*," I say, hoping for comforting words from Mama.

"I know," says Mama.

Boots looks quickly at Mama.

"Maggie? That sounds a little unkind."

A little.

"Oh," says Mama. "I didn't mean that."

Boots looks in the rearview mirror until he finds me.

I know him well enough to know what he is thinking.

It is this: *It's all right if you can't sing.*

All morning long we pass fields and rivers that are filled to their banks with water. We pass herds of cows and horses. We pass pigs and goats and farm meadows filled with sheep. It seems that Teddy has tired of calling everything he sees "cow." I turn to him as we pass the sheep.

"Baa, baa," I whisper.

Teddy smiles at me as if he knows it is a secret.

"Baa, baa," he says softly.

And then we see it.

The Red River.

Boots pulls the car over to park. Everyone is quiet.

The river is higher than some of the trees that border it. The river is flowing fast, carrying small trees along with it, tumbling pieces of what looks like roofs or small parts of sheds or porches.

"And there's the bridge we'll be crossing," says Boots softly.

The spidery metal bridge, painted red, crosses over to the farmland where Frankie lives. The river is so high it almost reaches the bridge. There is a policeman at either end, directing one car at a time to cross.

Boots starts the car.

"We'd better cross while we can," he says. "It's a long way around if the bridge closes."

The policeman waves us over the bridge.

"Go slowly, please," he says.

We cross the river slowly. I hold on to the door handle so tightly, my knuckles turn white. All around all I can see is water moving fast. It seems to want to carry us along with it, though I know we're on the bridge. No one talks in the car. When we finally reach the far side I realize I've been holding my breath. Boots drives the car up the hill past farms and meadows. I look back and it's still there, that river.

Boots has said that we have to help Frankie when the river floods her land. But how can we do that? We're just people, the five of us, and the river is fast and huge.

"Two more hours," says Boots very quietly. "We'll be at Frankie's in two hours."

"Boots?"

"What, Lucy?"

"I'm worried about the river."

"I am too. But, we'll do what we can."

"I'm worried about Frankie, too. She'll be mad at us for coming to her house."

"She'll be mad at me," Boots says.

"And me," says Mama. "Frankie would never be upset with you."

There is silence. We drive on, but when I turn around and look behind me, the river is always there.

"It will be all right," I say, looking at Teddy.

He looks at me steadily. Teddy isn't worried. I realize that I am talking to myself.

"It will," says Boots.

chapter 5

Frankie

Up a small hill, next to a herd of cows, then down a dirt road to the white house with the porch all around. Mama starts to cry.

The birdies fly away and they come back home.

Mama blows her nose.

The farmhouse faces the river. It is up the hill a bit, maybe midway, but the river is creeping up that hill. It has crossed the dirt road in one place and Boots drives up on the grass to avoid it. Farther up the hill men are piling up sandbags in front of the porch.

One of the men turns and it isn't a man at all. It's Frankie.

Mama opens the door and is out of the car before Boots comes to a stop. She runs to throw her arms around Frankie.

Frankie's long gray hair is braided and pinned over her head. She wears jeans and an old T-shirt. She's taller than Mama, and she stands quietly for a moment, not moving. Then, after a while, she puts her arms around Mama.

Gracie gets out of her car seat, and I climb back and undo Teddy. Boots gets out of the car and stretches. I hold Teddy's hands as he jumps down.

Gracie, Teddy, and I look out over the river.

Teddy points to the water.

"That is the river," I tell him. "River. It is not a cow."

Teddy looks at the river, then up at me.

He smiles suddenly.

"He knows," says Gracie.

Teddy knows the river isn't a cow.

"It is Teddy's joke," I say. "Isn't it, Teddy?"

"Teddy knows a lot more than we think he does," says Gracie.

I nod.

"He does."

Sometimes I think Teddy knows everything.

We eat dinner on Frankie's huge porch.

"You told me you weren't coming," says Frankie.

"Boots lied," says Gracie. "He knew you'd be mad at us."

Frankie smiles a little for the first time.

"'Lie' is a bit hard, don't you think?" says Frankie.

"Gracie is right," says Boots.

Frankie lifts her shoulders in a sigh.

She looks at Teddy and Gracie and me.

"I'm glad you're here," she says finally. "You can help. But," she adds, "don't forget that I have done this myself for many years. I am strong."

"And stubborn," says Gracie. "Mama says so."

Frankie bursts out laughing and we all relax.

There is one big table, a few smaller ones, wicker chairs and plants, and a hammock in one corner. Frankie has cooked a large ham, glazed with honey and brown sugar.

"I hope no one's a vegetarian," says Frankie.

"I'm thinking of it," says Gracie.

"Well, by the looks of the way you're eating that ham, I don't think you're ready yet," says Frankie.

She leans back and looks at the river.

"I want you all to be safe. That's why I told you not to come."

No one says anything. Except for Gracie.

"What can I do?" she asks.

Frankie turns to look at Gracie.

"You can help me keep an eye on her," she says.

"Her, who?" asks Boots.

"That river. She's a her in my book. She's been a friend most of these years, bringing boaters who deliver groceries. Bringing birds and beauty. We've lived through storms and sunrises and sunsets. Winter squalls. I want to see how far she's going to crawl up my hill. I want to know if she'll come into my house. Sometimes I talk to her at night. She's great company."

"Mom and Dad felt the same way," says Mama. "They always thought of the river as something more than a river."

"Cow," says Teddy all of a sudden.

"River," I say automatically.

Teddy points.

"Cow."

And there is a huge black cow with a white band around her middle wandering around the yard, scattering the chickens.

Boots stands up.

"Oh, my," he says.

I laugh.

"Boots likes that breed," I tell Frankie.

"*Loves* that breed," says Gracie.

"That's Becky," she says. "What are you doing out? I traded an old bull for her because I loved the way she looks. She's a great milker."

Frankie and Boots go down the steps to lead Becky back to the other cows.

"You're right, Teddy. That is a cow!" says Frankie.

"Dutch Belted," says Teddy in a loud voice.

Frankie turns around. So does Boots.

"I thought you told me Teddy doesn't talk!" says Frankie to Mama.

Mama's eyes widen. She shakes her head. And for the second time this day Mama bursts into tears.

"Yep," says Gracie to me, putting another piece of ham on her plate, "Teddy knows more than anyone thinks. Including words."

chapter 6

Rising Water

Frankie's house is large, with her bedroom downstairs on the river side. The rest of us choose our upstairs sleeping rooms. Gracie takes the room overlooking the fields and meadows. Mama and Boots choose the big back bedroom. When I go to bed, I see Boots standing at the moonlit window, looking out at the cows. Looking out at Becky. Teddy sleeps in the small bedroom next to mine. We put a gate at the top of the stairs "in case he walks in the night," Mama says.

I *know* he walks at night. I check that the gate is tightly closed when I go to my room. My room overlooks the growing river that, from my window, seems to cover everything in sight. It is still moving fast. I can see the water run by in the night.

And I see Frankie, standing by the river, tall and still. Maybe she is talking to her friend, the river. Maybe she is warning her.

When she turns to walk back up to the house, she looks up and sees me in the window before I can move away. She holds up her hand. I hold up mine.

Then she walks up the hill to the house. I hear the soft click of the front door.

"See?"

"Teddy."

I've been waiting for him.

Teddy touches me to make sure I'm there. There isn't moonlight now. The room is dark.

His little perfect voice sings. There are not many rugs upstairs and I wonder if the wood floors will carry his voice down the hall.

He sings "Are You Sleeping." I don't remember him singing that before, but I know Boots has sung it to him. He ends the song. He actually says the words "ding, ding, dong." Teddy is beginning to talk, even though he doesn't like to talk.

"Ding, ding, dong.
Ding, ding, dong."

He yawns.

I reach into my table drawer and take out a night-light. I take his hand and lead him back to his room. I plug in the light.

I cover him with a light blanket.

"Light," I tell him.

"Light," he whispers, and closes his eyes.

I wake to rain and voices and the sounds of people running down the stairs. I look out the window. The river has risen. Frankie is carrying bags of grain from the shed up the hill, away from the water.

I get out of bed and pull on my jeans and shirt. I look in on Teddy. He is still sleeping.

I unhook the gate, making sure it is latched again, and run downstairs. I open the door and run outside.

"I'll help," I tell Frankie.

She dumps two bags in a wheel-barrow.

"You can wheel it up to the big barn," she says. "Then come back for more."

I start off, but the earth is soft from

rain so I have to push harder. The wheels sink a bit in the dirt, and I'm pushing uphill.

Boots comes and helps me push. His hair is plastered to his head with rain. We wheel up the hill to the barn without speaking. We go into the dark barn and Boots takes the bags out of the wheelbarrow and places them up on high wooden platforms.

"What's happening?" I ask.

"The grain was delivered to the shed by mistake. The water is rising there."

"It will reach the porch, won't it," I say.

Boots nods.

We hurry back down the hill.

"Where's Teddy?"

"Sleeping. I hitched the gate."

Boots nods.

"Your mama's up there anyway."

A man is helping Frankie drag out more grain bags. He smiles at me, but doesn't speak.

This time Frankie helps me with the wheelbarrow.

"So, is that your boyfriend?" I ask her as we push up the soggy lawn.

"Better than a boyfriend," says Frankie with a laugh. "A friend."

A gust of wind blows my hair across my face.

When we go into the barn I see the chickens up on a shelf of hay: Ella and Sofia and Nickel. They look very peaceful.

"Mama says chickens only get excited

when they feel like it. On their own terms, Mama says."

"Looks like she's right. We should be that lucky," says Frankie.

Gracie comes out and we wheel more grain up the hill until finally we have moved all of it.

Some men have come to pile more sandbags in front of the house. We sit on the porch, watching. Frankie carries a big pot of coffee out to the porch.

"Lucy, could you bring out a tray of cups?"

I go into the big kitchen. It is dry and warm. Mama and Teddy sit at the table sharing toast.

"See?" says Teddy.

"Teddy."

"How is it out there?" asks Mama.

"Wet. And"—I look at Mama—"the river's rising. It will come up to the porch."

Mama nods with a tired look as if she's been through this all before. And she has.

"Mama?"

She looks up.

"Does the river scare you?"

"Always," says Mama.

I put cups on a big tray, put the sugar bowl on, and get cream out of the refrigerator.

Mama and Teddy follow me to the porch. Frankie's friend is there.

"Louis!" says Mama happily.

She puts her arms around him.

"Nice family," says Louis.

Mama smiles.

"I've known Louis my whole life," she says.

"And mine," says Louis crisply.

I hand him coffee and he sits down, taking off his rain hat.

Teddy walks over to him and puts his hand on Louis's knee.

"Hello," says Louis.

"That's Teddy, who doesn't care much about talking," says Mama.

"Me too," says Louis.

"Too," says Teddy.

"He talks," says Louis.

"He has other great qualities," says Gracie.

Louis smiles.

"Me too," he says.

"He knows more than people think he does," she says.

"Me too," says Louis.

"Too," repeats Teddy.

The men have piled up sandbags and gone home. We're cleaning up the kitchen. Louis sits at the kitchen table, Teddy still staring at him.

"Teddy, let Louis be," says Mama.

"It's fine," says Louis. "I never get this much adoration from Frankie."

Frankie grins at Louis.

"I'll come back tomorrow," says Louis. "We might be all right if the rain stops. If it doesn't, we might have to move first-floor furniture upstairs."

"Oh no," says Frankie, sitting at the table.

"We can do that," says Boots. "I think I may roll up the rugs tonight and carry them upstairs. Might save time if it gets rough."

Louis nods.

"Glad you're here."

"Louis and I moved the cows to the upper field," says Frankie. "There's a small barn up there for shelter. There are only six of them."

"If Boots could he'd move Becky right into the kitchen," I say.

"Ah, Becky. She is quite spectacular," says Louis, nodding. He says the word "spectacular" slowly.

"Spec-tac-u," says Teddy.

Mama puts her hands over her mouth.

"No crying, Maggie," says Boots.

"Spec-tac-u-lar," Louis says to Teddy.

"Yay!" says Teddy, his arms in the air.

Even Louis laughs.

chapter 7

Waiting for the Flood

The rugs are all upstairs, lying in neat rolls in the wide hallway. We have moved up some of the furniture. "You should move upstairs too," Mama says to Frankie.

"Not until I have to," says Frankie.

I follow Frankie as she goes to the

hallway and puts on her raincoat and hat. She smiles at me.

"If I sleep upstairs I won't be able to hear Teddy sing to you," she whispers to me.

She sees the look on my face and puts her arm around me.

"There is a vent in the floor in your room that goes to my room. Don't worry. I can tell it is something between you and Teddy. A secret."

She opens the door.

"Does he come to sing to you every night?"

I nod.

"And no one else?"

I nod again.

"It made me happy. It made me cry,"

she says as she goes out the door to talk to the river.

The rain goes on.

I hope Teddy comes into my room again tonight.

I hope he sings for Frankie.

Upstairs, I take out my notebook. My page is blank except for one line.

The Ring-Around Cow.

I write.

Big black night sky body.

There is a wavery moon outside my window because of the rain.

I write.

Wrapped in the moon.

I can't write anymore. But I know that this won't be a rhymed poem. That is too slim for what I want to say.

It is too slim for the cow.

Tomorrow I have to go look at the spectacular Becky. If it isn't raining. If there isn't a flood.

I go down the hallway. Mama and Boots's door is closed. Gracie is sleeping. Teddy looks at me, his eyes gleaming in the night light. I go into his room and kiss him good night.

"Teddy?"

"See."

I smile because we have reversed the way we usually talk. Teddy smiles because he knows it too.

"I love you, Teddy."

"Love," says Teddy, his voice faint with sleep.

He holds my hand, and I sit on his bed for a while, until I know it is all right to take my hand away.

In my room I look out the window. In the moonlight I can see the water is slipping over the sandbags. Frankie stands there, her arms crossed. She is probably cross with her friend, the river.

When she turns and walks back to the house, she doesn't look up to my window.

In the night the rain falls harder. I hear a door open upstairs, then footsteps on the stairs going down. It is probably Boots. Then I turn over and see Teddy.

He stands in the doorway, looking at me.

"See?"

"Teddy."

I wait, but Teddy doesn't sing. He comes over and crawls into my bed.

"Teddy? It's rain. Only rain. It's all right."

He looks at me and waits.

And suddenly I know what he wants.

"I can't sing, Teddy. I can't," I say. "You sing."

Teddy puts his hand up to my mouth.

I sigh.

"What do you want?"

"'Baa, Baa,'" he says, almost in a whisper.

I hope Frankie isn't downstairs listening to my terrible singing.

Teddy waits. He puts his hand up to my mouth again.

I sing for Teddy.

I finish the song.

*"One for my master, and one
for my dame,
and one for the little boy who lives
in the lane."*

Teddy smiles. He likes my singing. He doesn't even know I *can't* sing.

Then he turns over and looks at me.

And he sings "Baa, Baa," so sweetly in the night that if Frankie is listening she'll weep.

When he finishes his song, he turns over again, and I know that he will sleep with me. I don't mind. I like his warm little body next to me while it is raining outside the window.

"Baa, baa, See," Teddy says.

"Baa, baa, Teddy," I say.

And he curls up next to me like a small dog.

The rain falls. The river rises.

But we are safe inside.

chapter 8

Friend

All night long I hear different things— the hard rain and wind outside, and the soft breathing of Teddy next to me. Then, near morning, something changes. I lift my head off the pillow.

The rain has stopped.

We all wake early. It isn't light yet.

There is just a pale slice of light low above the land. Mama, Boots, and I go downstairs together. Gracie takes Teddy's hand and they walk slowly down the stairs. We hear the sound of a far-away motor.

Frankie comes out of her bedroom, braiding her long hair, her robe flapping.

"Well, let's see," she says to us.

She opens the door.

And there is an ocean of river, as far as we can see. It is not quiet, still water. It moves fast, small boards and the tops of some trees going past and tumbling into the yard.

Beside me Mama gasps. Boots takes her hand. The river has come up the hill and swept away the porch steps. Water sits even with the porch floor.

I understand for the first time why Mama was always scared about the river.

As we watch, the small shed at the foot of the hill moves and tips. And then it is carried away by the river. As the sun rises, the morning light shines everywhere, reflected by all the water. And then we see something else.

At the far end of the porch is Becky. She is eating flowers out of the blue painted flower box. She stops to look up at us, still chewing, then goes back to her food.

"Dutch Belted," says Teddy behind me.

Frankie laughs at Teddy and at Becky.

"Becky, you're a clever girl. How did you get here?"

Boots goes over to rub her neck, and Becky brushes against him happily, still chewing pansies. I move closer to Becky, and she lifts her head to look at me. She stares at me, stopping her chewing, as if thinking her own thoughts.

Her eyes.

Her eyes are so big I can see my own reflection there, looking tiny next to this huge cow.

The motor noise comes closer. It is Louis, standing at the tiller of his motorboat, coming carefully closer and cutting the motor.

"Why, Louis, you look almost heroic," says Frankie.

"You're quite a sight yourself, Frankie," he says.

Her braids still hang down.

"Is everyone all right?" he calls. "You lost your steps."

"We're fine," calls Frankie. "How is it out there?"

"Bridge is closed. Moody's porch was carried away too, and part of Lester's barn."

"Then we're better off than many," says Frankie.

"Word is that the danger is over. No more rain in sight," says Louis.

"Good," says Frankie.

"And I see you've got a porch cow," says Louis. "Floated in, did she?"

Boots laughs. "I'll get my boots and

take her down the back steps where the water isn't so high."

"Becky almost made it to the kitchen," says Mama, making Boots smile.

Boots gets his boots. He slips a line around Becky's neck. They start to walk down the porch. Suddenly, Becky stops and turns her head to look at me.

Those eyes.

Then she clumps off the porch, down the back steps into a foot of water. I watch Boots lead her up the hill to the barn, where the other cows wait.

"Louis," says Teddy very clearly.

"Teddy," says Louis.

"What can I bring you when I come for dinner?" asks Louis.

"Did I invite you?" asks Frankie.

"You meant to," says Louis.

"We have ham and salad and beans. The stove still works—I made coffee. Milk and bread would be nice."

Louis nods.

"Louis," says Teddy again.

"Teddy doesn't even say 'mama,' yet he says 'Louis,'" says Mama.

"That's because he and Louis are alike. Louis doesn't say much most times. Can you sing, Louis?" asks Frankie, smiling at me. I know our secret—Teddy's and Frankie's and mine—is safe. Louis pushes the boat away from the house with an oar.

He sings.

"You take the high road, and I'll take
the low road,
And I'll be in Scotland before ye."

His voice is steady and clear. He starts the motor and goes slowly off.

Frankie grins.

"He sings!"

She pins her braids neatly over her head.

"Who knew?" she says, amazed.

"Maybe you should marry him," says Gracie.

"I don't need to marry him," says Frankie.

She goes close to the edge of the porch and looks at the river.

"Thank you for not coming into my house, old friend," she says loudly. "Thank you."

Two ducks suddenly flutter into the yard, skidding to a stop in the water. They float happily.

No one speaks.

"Thank you for that, too," she says in a soft voice.

Then, after a moment, Frankie turns and goes into the house.

chapter 9

Darkness and Light

We have bacon and eggs and biscuits for breakfast.

"Bacon and ham in one day," Frankie says to Gracie. "Not yet a vegetarian?"

"Nope," says Gracie.

"I was once," says Mama.

"I remember," says Frankie. "You were lots of things."

Mama sighs.

"I was going to be lots of things. Coming back here reminds me of all those things I meant to be."

"And you came to Boston to go to school, and you met me and fell in love, and look at you!" says Boots.

"Look at me," repeats Mama.

There is a small silence at the table.

"And you have Boots, and Grace, and Lucy, and Teddy," says Frankie.

"And Langhorne Slim," I add.

Mama gets up, taking her plate to the sink to rinse. She goes out of the kitchen, through the hallway, and out to the porch.

"Maybe I shouldn't have said that," I say.

Boots gets up.

"No, it isn't you. Mama needs something all her own, that's all," he says.

He goes out to where Mama is.

"Mama needs more than us," I say.

"Not really," says Frankie. "She just doesn't quite know what she has. She never did. She'll find that out one day. I promise."

Frankie pours coffee and leans over close to me.

"Baa, baa, See," she says softly.

I look quickly at her.

"You heard last night?"

Frankie nods.

"You know I can't sing then," I say.

"That doesn't matter. What matters is that you are a spectacular sister."

Teddy looks up.

"Spec-tac-u," he says.

"What are you two talking about?" asks Gracie.

"Secrets," says Frankie. "Don't you have secrets too?"

"Lots of them," says Gracie happily.

"Lucky girl," says Frankie. "You're spectacular too."

"Spec-tac-u-lar!" says Teddy slowly.

He looks all around the table at us, waiting.

"Yay!" we all shout, our arms in the air. Even Frankie.

Frankie leans over to ask a question.

"Who is Langhorne Slim?"

Gracie and I laugh out loud.

Slowly, during the day, the river calms a bit. There are fewer pieces of trees flowing by. The water begins to fall away from the porch, leaving watermarks behind. There is still a foot of water in the backyard, but the sun is bright and warm.

Boots and Frankie go up to the barn to milk the cows. Mama goes with them, carrying Teddy up through the water to dry land to feed her chickens. The chickens have come out in the sunlight, walking around in the grasses.

Gracie sits on the porch with her drawing pad, sketching scenes of the wide river and the ducks. Her drawing of the big Dutch Belted cow lies on the table.

"This is beautiful, Gracie."

"Thanks. It's simple to draw. Like someone else made this big, big drawing and all I had to do was fill it in."

I stare at Gracie.

I sit down and stare at her drawing.

"You're brilliant, Gracie," I tell her.

Gracie looks up from her drawing and smiles at me.

"I'm only six," she says. "Too young to be brilliant."

She goes back to her work. I go upstairs and into my room. The bed is still rumpled from sleep—dents made from Teddy's body, my body. I pull up the covers and smooth us away.

I pick up my notebook.

I write.

Ring-Around Cow

> *What artist*
> *Sketched*
> *Sculpted*
> *Your*
> > *Big black sky body*

I look at the page for a long time. Boots is right. You can't write anything better than a cow. I tear out the page of the notebook. I close the notebook.

And that is when I hear Mama's screaming.

chapter 10

Teddy

The screams go on. I drop my notebook, the poem page flying across the floor. I run downstairs. Gracie and I run into each other as she comes in from the porch.

"What?" I ask.

"Mama," Gracie says. "I don't know."

We run through the kitchen. The

teakettle is screaming too. I turn off the stove, and out the window I see Boots and Frankie running through the water up to the barn.

Gracie and I race out the door and through the water in our sneakers. The water is cold.

Mama stands at the top of the hill calling, "Teddy! Teddy!"

My whole body turns cold. My heart pounds.

"It's Teddy."

Gracie starts to sob. Tears come down her face. We get to the end of the water and we run up the green grass to the barn. Boots takes Mama by the arms. He shakes her to stop her screaming and crying.

"Which way did he go?" he says very loudly.

Mama shakes her head.

"He was right here with the chickens. I went in the barn to get more chicken food. And when I came out he wasn't here."

Boots turns to Frankie.

"Where would he go? What's in the meadow? Are there cow paths? Tell me!" he almost shouts at Frankie.

"There are cow paths. He could get under the fence and wander," says Frankie. "How long has he been gone?"

Mama shakes her head.

"Ten minutes maybe. I don't know! It wasn't a long time I left him. It wasn't!"

Mama begins to cry.

Gracie goes to the fence.

"Teddy! Teddy!" she calls.

There is no answer.

"We can't stay here," says Mama, her voice hysterical with fear.

"If he follows the fence, where will he come out?" Boots asks Frankie quickly.

"Little River," says Mama, suddenly calm.

"Little River?"

Frankie nods.

"We call it Little River, but it is more like a stream most of the time. It cuts back behind the meadow, a very small arm of it."

Boots starts running along the fence and we follow him. I put my hand to my face and feel tears.

"Teddy!" shouts Boots. "Teddy! Where are you?"

Mama starts to follow, but Boots stops her.

"Stay there in case he comes back, Maggie!" he shouts. "He needs to find someone home!"

Mama stops as if she's been slapped.

Gracie and I run behind Frankie. We all call Teddy's name over and over and over. We run through the woods that border the meadow. Cows lift their heads to watch us.

"The water's ahead," shouts Frankie.

We run into a clearing where the stream cuts through a steep bank. The water is running over and around rocks.

"The small dam is that way," Frankie says to Boots. "It's kind of old, and once in a while rocks fall out and more water gets through."

"Teddy! Teddy!"

Frankie stops suddenly and grabs my arm.

"Wait!" she says.

Everyone stops.

"Sing, Lucy!" says Frankie. "Sing!"

"You know I can't sing!" I shout.

Frankie shakes me like Boots shook Mama.

"He sings to you every night," she says. "If he hears you he'll answer. You're the one he sings to!"

I walk to the edge of the water.

"Lucy," says Boots. "Sing."

I've never heard his voice so stern.
I open my mouth. And I sing.

"The birdies fly away, and they come
back home.
The birdies fly away, and they come
back home."

My voice breaks and Boots beckons
me to go on.

"Fly away, fly away,
All the birdies fly away.
The birdies fly away, and they come
back home."

I stop. There is no answer.
"Again," says Boots in a strong voice.

"The birdies fly away, and they come
back home.
The birdies fly away, and they come
back home."

A small, perfect voice answers. *Teddy's*
voice.

"Fly away, fly away,
All the birdies fly away.
The birdies fly away, and they come
back home."

Teddy is singing the words!
Boots has already run toward the
sound. We run after him. The stream
seems higher and faster, as if filling up
from somewhere.

"Sing more, Lucy!" calls Boots.

I sing and when we reach a bend in the stream, there is Teddy. He has scrambled down the steep bank and is in the middle of the stream, sitting on a rock.

Boots looks like he might cry. He slides down the bank, dirt and stones falling with him.

Teddy looks at me as Boots walks into the rising stream, struggling though the water.

"Sing," says Gracie softly. "It will keep Teddy quiet."

"The birdies fly away, and they come
back home.
The birdies fly away, and they come
back home."

Boots slips and falls, gets up again.
Teddy sings.

"Fly away, fly away,
All the birdies fly away."

Boots reaches Teddy and puts his
arms around him, holding him tightly as
he makes his way back.

I'm crying too hard to sing with
Teddy.

Frankie puts her arm around me.
Gracie holds my hand, something she
has never done before.

Ever.

Teddy is glad to see us and is not crying,
as if he has expected all along that we'd

find him. He has scrapes and bug bites, a bloody knee, but he is smiling. He has lost a red sneaker. He points to his bare foot with a sad sound.

"It's all right, Teddy," says Boots. "We'll get you new sneakers."

Boots's voice breaks.

"He must have walked out into the stream when there wasn't so much water," says Frankie.

Once, as we walk back along the river and through the trees to the meadow, Teddy reaches up and touches the tears on Boots's face.

"See?"

"Teddy," I say.

He smiles at our ritual.

"You were brave," says Gracie to me.

"Brave?"

"You sang," says Gracie.

I start to laugh and can't stop. I don't know why I'm laughing. It just seems funny to me that I am brave because I sing badly.

"You saved Teddy," says Gracie.

"You did," says Boots.

"You did," says Frankie, who is finally crying herself.

I think about Mama. I think about how guilty she feels that Teddy wandered off. She feels bad that she couldn't help find him. She will worry about how Teddy feels about her.

We walk along the meadow fence.

"Cow," says Teddy, pointing.

"Cow," I say.

Teddy sees Mama standing at the end of the fence. She isn't crying. She is all cried out.

Teddy smiles at her. He reaches out his arms and calls to her.

"Mama! Mama!"

Boots hands Teddy over and Teddy puts his arms around Mama's neck. Mama doesn't say anything. She holds on to Teddy and carries him down the lawn, through the water, to the house.

Suddenly, Boots's knees sag.

"Boots!"

Frankie takes his arm and helps him sit on the grass. She sits next to him. Gracie and I sit on the other side.

"Tired," says Boots.

He is quiet.

"Tired," he repeats after a moment, as if it is the only word he has the energy to say.

He lies back and puts his arm over his eyes.

And it is then we see a stream of blood on Boots's cheek from a cut.

Frankie hands me a handkerchief.

I put it on Boots's cheek and hold it over the cut. After a moment Boots puts his hand over mine and holds it there.

"Lucy, I kept your secret until I couldn't anymore," says Frankie.

"I know. That's all right."

It is quiet again.

Then Boots speaks without moving.

"I heard that sweet little voice slipping through the darkness one night. I just didn't know it was Teddy."

Boots may be a farmer, but he is still a poet.

chapter 11

Poet

Louis ties his boat to the porch and jumps up and climbs over the railing.

"You could have worn my waders," says Frankie.

"They are women's waders," says Louis.

"They are not," says Frankie crossly.

We laugh.

"I'll build you new steps when the water is gone," says Louis.

"No," says Frankie loudly. "I'll build them myself."

Louis sighs.

"Frankie," he says softly. "Remember arithmetic? Remember measuring? Remember the bench you made? Arithmetic?"

He says "arithmetic" slowly: a-rith-me-tic.

"Oh," says Frankie.

She is very quiet.

Teddy walks up close to Louis.

"Louis," he says.

"Teddy," says Louis.

"A-rith-me-tic," says Teddy.

I watch Mama and she doesn't care that Teddy said "Louis" or "arithmetic." Teddy said "Mama" today. Mama looks different somehow. The edges of her face are softer. There is a sort of quiet about her.

"What about the bench?" I ask.

"Nothing," says Louis. He smiles. "Only that one end was much higher than the other."

Even Frankie laughs.

Louis looks around the kitchen where everyone sits.

"What did you all do today? What happened to your cheek, Boots?"

We tell Louis about Teddy walking away.

"Where was he?"

"He was at Little River," says Frankie.

"In the middle of the water. Sitting on a rock."

Teddy pulls up his jeans and shows Louis his bandage.

"He knows what we're talking about," says Gracie.

"Of course he does," says Mama. "He may be the smartest little boy in the universe."

Louis holds out his hand to Teddy. Teddy takes it.

"How did you find him?" asks Louis.

"Lucy sang," says Gracie.

"Sang?"

"Teddy sings to Lucy. He loves to sing to Lucy," says Gracie.

"So you thought Teddy might answer Lucy."

"And he did," says Boots.

"He wandered away from me," says Mama to Louis, as if confessing something terrible.

Louis smiles.

"My little sister Janie disappeared one day for seven hours. We found her in the barn, sleeping in the hay. It took a long time for my mother to forgive herself. It was her secret guilt."

"Secrets," says Boots.

He holds up my notebook paper with the poem written there.

"Is this another of your secrets, Lucy?"

I take a deep breath.

"Where did you find that?" I ask.

"Blowing down the upstairs hallway, from your room to my room," says Boots.

"Almost as if it was saying to me, 'Pick me up and read me.'"

Boots says "Pick me up and read me" in a funny high voice I've never heard before. It makes me smile.

"Did you read it?" I ask.

Boots shakes his head.

I sigh. "I wanted to write you a poem to make you happy. I wanted to write a cow poem. You said cows were poetry. That you couldn't write a poem better than a cow."

"I remember saying that."

"And you were right," I say. "No one can write a poem better than a cow."

I look at the paper in his hand.

"I meant to throw that away," I say.

Boots nods.

"I know about that, believe me," he says. "May I read it before you do it?"

I shrug my shoulders.

Boots reads my poem to himself. It seems to me to take a very long time. But that is because no one speaks. The room is filled with silence.

Boots stares at the page for a long time. Finally, I realize he doesn't know what to say. I reach out for the paper, but he holds the page against his chest.

"This is a beautiful, intelligent poem, Lucy," Boots says.

"It is?"

"Yes, it is. And, Lucy?"

"What?"

"I was wrong. You have written a poem as beautiful as a cow."

I don't want to cry in front of everyone.

"I never wrote about her eyes," I whisper.

"You will write another poem," says Boots.

"Maybe we could hear the poem," says Louis shyly.

I have forgotten about everybody else in the room. I don't care if anyone else hears the poem. I only care what Boots thinks of it.

Boots sits at the kitchen table and reads.

"Ring-Around Cow

What artist
Sketched
Sculpted

Your
> *Big black sky body*
> *Wrapped in the moon*
>> *So you carry both*
>> *Darkness*
>> *And Day,*
>> *Shadow*
>> *And Light."*

It is very quiet when Boots finishes reading. He puts the paper on the table.

Finally Frankie stands up.

"Another of your secrets is revealed," she says to me.

Boots nods.

"You're a poet, Lucy."

Everyone has gone to bed after raucous and embarrassing dancing to Langhorne Slim because Frankie wanted us to dance.

"We are fools!" says Mama, laughing and laughing as she dances. And we are.

I am not sure I can sleep tonight. I keep thinking about Teddy, lost and in danger. I keep thinking about Mama, scared and guilty because Teddy wandered off when she wasn't watching. Mostly I think I won't sleep because I'm a poet. I have heard poets don't sleep very much and are miserable a good part of the time.

It is nighttime and Teddy has not come to my bedroom. Maybe, since our secret is out, he won't come here anymore. Maybe he'll go to Mama's room. Maybe he will sleep all night because of his long, long day. I miss him and

I'm sad. Maybe this is part of being a miserable poet.

I go to sleep, hearing the soft midnight chime of the hall clock.

"See?"

My eyes pop open.

"Teddy."

There is a moon and I can see his eyes. He finds my hand and begins to sing.

"The birdies fly away, and they come
    back home.
The birdies fly away, and they come
    back home."

I don't hear at first, but Teddy does. He pulls my hand and I get out of bed. We walk *out into the hallway. Teddy sings. From all the bedrooms come the sounds of singing, too.*

*"Fly away, fly away,
All the birdies fly away.
The birdies fly away, and they come
back home."*

The voices sound peaceful and sweet and quiet, the way a hymn sometimes sounds in an old church with wood floors.

I lead Teddy back to his bed. I cover him up to his chin.

"See?"

"Teddy."

I kiss him good night and smooth his hair. He is asleep before I leave the room.

I climb back into my own bed. I will sleep now, I know. Teddy sang to me. I am no longer a miserable poet.

I am just a poet.

Patricia MacLachlan

is the author of many well-loved novels and picture books, including *Sarah, Plain and Tall*, winner of the Newbery Medal; its sequels, *Skylark* and *Caleb's Story*; *Waiting for the Magic*; *Edward's Eyes*; *The True Gift*; and *White Fur Flying*. She is a board member of the National Children's Book and Literacy Alliance. She lives in western Massachusetts.